JACK
and the
FLUMFLUM
TREE

For Corin, Keelan and Aiden – J.D.
For Susie Barrie – D.R.

First published 2011 by Macmillan Children's Books
This edition published 2012 by Macmillan Children's Books
a division of Macmillan Publishers Limited
20 New Wharf Road, London N1 9RR
Basingstoke and Oxford
Associated companies throughout the world
www.panmacmillan.com

ISBN: 978-1-4472-2744-1

Text copyright © Julia Donaldson 2011
Illustrations copyright © David Roberts 2011

1 3 5 7 9 8 6 4 2

A CIP catalogue record for this book
is available from the British Library.

Printed in Belgium

Written by

JULIA DONALDSON

Illustrated by

DAVID ROBERTS

JACK
and the
FLUMFLUM
TREE

MACMILLAN CHILDREN'S BOOKS

Jack had a granny and his granny had spots,
Great big purple ones, lots and lots.

The doctor came and he shook his head.
"Your granny has the moozles," the doctor said.
"And the only cure in the world," said he,
"Is the fruit that grows on the flumflum tree,
And the only place that the flumflum grows
Is the faraway Isle of Blowyernose."

So Jack built a boat, and Jack found a crew –

Red-cheeked Rose and stubble-cheeked Stu –
And he said to Stu, and he said to Rose,
"We're off to the Isle of Blowyernose."

Granny came down to the dock with Jack,
And she gave him a bulgy patchwork sack.
And in that sack were a pair of wooden spoons,
A porridge bowl, tent pegs, some red and blue balloons,
Granny's old skipping rope, a pack of chewing gum,
Three spotty hankies and a tom-tom drum.
And Jack said, "Granny, what *is* the use of those?"
"Aha," said Granny, and she tapped her nose.

Then off sailed Jack, with Stu and Rose,
For the faraway Isle of Blowyernose.

"Sharks!" cried Rose.
"Lots!" cried Stu.

"They'll gobble us! They'll guzzle us! Whatever shall we do?"

"Don't get your knickers in a twist," said Jack.
"Let's have a look in the patchwork sack."

"Red balloons! Blue balloons! They should do the trick!
Puff, puff, blow 'em up, let 'em go, quick!"
Then the sharks went NIP and the sharks went GNASH,
Chasing those balloons with a BANG, POP, SPLASH!

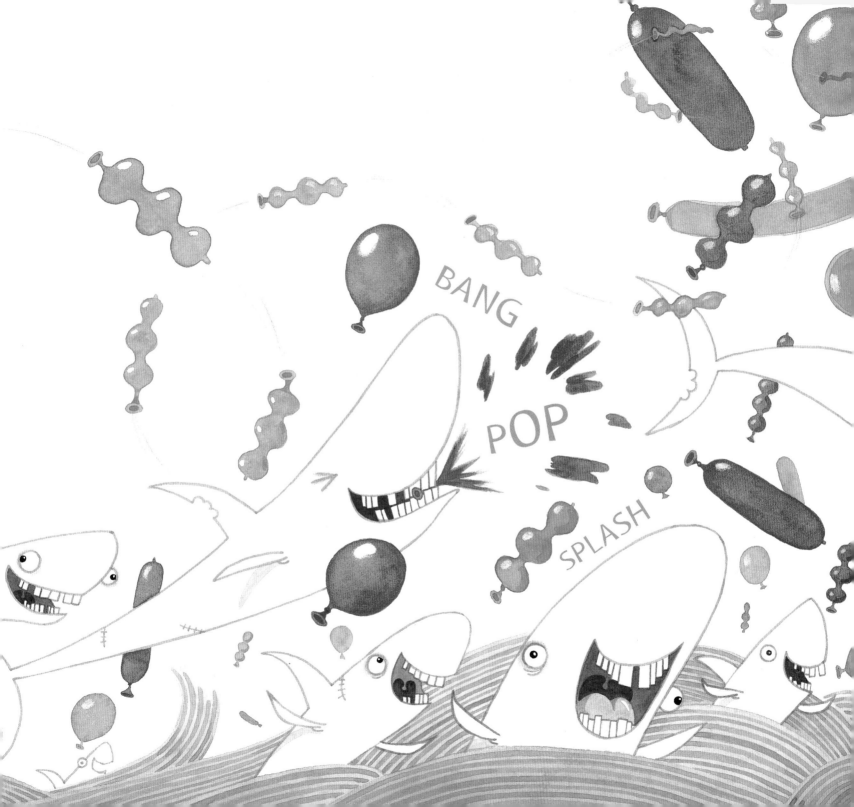

"A leak!" cried Rose.
"It's wet!" cried Stu.
"The boat is full of water. Whatever shall we do?"

"Don't get your knickers in a twist," said Jack.
"Let's have a look in the patchwork sack."

"Granny's pack of chewing gum!
That should do the trick.
Chew it up, stretch it out,
stick it in quick!"

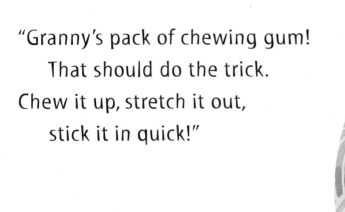

So they chewed and they stretched
and they plugged that hole,

And they baled out the water
with Granny's porridge bowl.

Then on sailed Jack, with Stu and Rose,
For the faraway Isle of Blowyernose.

"Whoops!" cried Rose.
"Help!" cried Stu.
"I can't swim for toffee! Whatever will you do?"

"Don't get your knickers in a twist!" said Jack.
"Let's have a look in the patchwork sack."

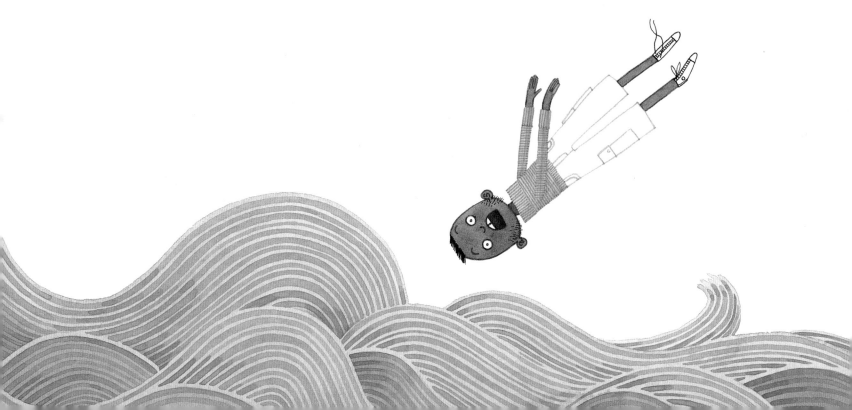

"Granny's old skipping rope!
That should do the trick.
Hold tight, throw it out,
grab the handle quick!"

So they heaved and they hauled
and they pulled Stu in.
"Good old Granny!
She's saved my skin!"

Then on sailed Jack, with Stu and Rose,
Till they came to the Isle of Blowyernose.

And there on a hill, for all to see,
Stood the bright green feathery flumflum tree.

"It's tall!" cried Rose.
"It's smooth!" cried Stu.
"It's not got any branches! Whatever shall we do?"

"Don't get your knickers in a twist," said Jack.
"Let's have a look in the patchwork sack."

"Granny's bag of tent pegs! They should do the trick!
Bang, bang, knock 'em in, climb the tree quick!"

Then up went Rose, as nimble as could be
And she brought down the fruit of the flumflum tree.

Then Jack and Stu and
Rose had a doze
On the soft sandy beach
of Blowyernose.

"A thief!" cried Rose.
"A monkey!" yelled Stu.
"He's got our precious flumflum! Whatever shall we do?"

"Don't get your knickers in a twist," said Jack.
"Let's have a look in the patchwork sack."

"Granny's spoons and tom-tom! They should do the trick!
Pick 'em up, thump thump, sing a song quick!"

The monkey crept closer.
   He listened to the tunes.
He put down the flumflum
   and he grabbed the wooden spoons.

Then back sailed Jack,
   with Stu and Rose,
All the way home
   from Blowyernose.

Granny ate the flumflum. The moozles disappeared.
"She's cured!" said the doctor, and everyone cheered.

And Jack said, "Thank you for the pair of wooden spoons,
The porridge bowl, the skipping rope, the red and blue balloons.
Thank you for the tent pegs and the pack of chewing gum,
And thank you, Granny, for the tom-tom drum . . .

But the three spotty hankies —
what *was* the use of those?"

"The hankies, silly, were to
blow your nose!"